THE SECRET HIDDEN SCROLLS

BOOK NINE
THE FINAL SCROLL

BY M. J. THOMAS

WORTHY
kids™

For my Lord and Savior, Jesus! Thank you for taking me
on this amazing adventure!

—M.J.T.

ISBN: 978-1-5460-3435-3

WorthyKids
Hachette Book Group
1290 Avenue of the Americas
New York, NY 10104

Library of Congress Cataloging-in-Publication Data
Names: Thomas, M. J., 1969- author.
Title: The final scroll / by M.J. Thomas.
Description: New York, NY : WorthyKids, [2021] | Series: The secret of the
   hidden scrolls ; book 9 | Audience: Ages 6-9. | Summary: Peter, Mary,
   and Hank travel back to Jerusalem during the height of Jesus' popularity
   where they discover the religious leaders have hatched a plan that
   causes one of Jesus' disciples to betray him, and now with time running
   out, Peter and Mary must solve the secret of the scroll before they get
   stuck in the past forever.
Identifiers: LCCN 2020040714 | ISBN 9781546034353 (paperback)
Subjects: CYAC: Time travel—Fiction. | Jesus Christ—Fiction. |
   Scrolls—Fiction. | Brothers and sisters—Fiction. | Dogs—Fiction. |
   Jerusalem—History—1st century—Fiction.
Classification: LCC PZ7.1.T4654 F56 | DDC [Fic]—dc23
LC record available at https://lccn.loc.gov/2020040714

Cover illustration by Graham Howells
Interior illustrations by Daniel Hawkins
Designed by Georgina Chidlow-Irvin

Lexile® level 450L

Printed and bound in the U.S.A.
CW
10 9 8 7 6 5 4 3 2

CONTENTS

PROLOGUE

Nine-year-old Peter and his ten-year-old sister, Mary, stood at the door to the huge, old house and waved as their parents drove away. Peter and Mary and their dog, Hank, would be spending the month with Great-Uncle Solomon.

Peter thought it would be the most boring month ever—until he realized Great-Uncle Solomon was an archaeologist. Great-Uncle Solomon showed them artifacts and treasures and told them stories about his travels around the globe. And then he shared his most amazing discovery of all—the Legend of the Hidden Scrolls! These weren't just dusty old scrolls. They held secrets—and they would lead to travel through time.

Soon Peter, Mary, and Hank were flung back in time to important moments in the Bible. They witnessed the Creation of the earth and helped Noah load the ark. They endured plagues in Egypt and stood on the walls of Jericho. They watched David battle Goliath and faced lions with Daniel. They met the new King, Jesus, and watched him perform miracles. They had exciting adventures, all while trying to solve the secrets in the scrolls.

Now Peter and Mary are ready for their *final* adventure . . . as soon as they hear the lion's roar.

The Legend of the Hidden Scrolls
THE SCROLLS CONTAIN THE TRUTH YOU SEEK.
BREAK THE SEAL. UNROLL THE SCROLL.
AND YOU WILL SEE THE PAST UNFOLD.
AMAZING ADVENTURES ARE IN STORE
FOR THOSE WHO FOLLOW THE LION'S ROAR!

1

ONE LAST ADVENTURE

Peter placed the gold medallions side-by-side on the top of the dresser in his bedroom at Great-Uncle Solomon's house. The eight medallions sparkled in the sunlight streaming in from the window over his unmade bed.

Peter ran his finger across the imprints on the large gold coins. He felt the outline of a tree, Noah's ark, a pyramid, the Ark of the Covenant, a crown, a lion, a star, and a heart. He thought about each of the adventures.

The bedroom door swung open, and his big

sister Mary rushed in with Hank. She pointed to the empty suitcase on his bed.

"You haven't started packing?" said Mary. "Mom and Dad will be back any minute."

Hank nudged Peter's leg. Peter bent over to pet the dog's head.

"I guess I better hurry," said Peter, tossing some jeans and socks into his suitcase.

"Aren't you excited to see Mom and Dad?" said Mary.

Peter plopped down on the edge of the bed. "I am. But I'm going to miss Great-Uncle Solomon and our adventures back in time."

"Me too," said Mary.

Peter snapped his fingers. "Maybe we have time for one more adventure!"

"*Woof!*" Hank spun around and wagged his tail.

Mary looked at the suitcase and twisted her

hair. "I don't know. Mom and Dad will be back soon, and you need to finish."

Peter grabbed the rest of his shorts, shirts, socks, and underwear in one big armful and tossed them in the suitcase. "There, I'm packed! Let's go on an adventure!"

"We can't," said Mary. "We have to wait to hear the lion's roar."

"That's true," said Peter. "But we can at least explore Great-Uncle Solomon's house."

"I think we've already seen everything," said Mary.

"No," said Peter. "We haven't been in the tower in the back corner of the house."

"That's right," said Mary. "You asked Great-Uncle Solomon about the tower when we were walking to the barn."

Peter raised his eyebrows. "I wonder what's up there?"

Mary's eyes twinkled. He knew she couldn't resist a mystery.

"Come on," said Peter. "Let's find out!"

"Okay, but we have to hurry!" said Mary.

"We will," said Peter, grabbing the brown leather adventure bag. "Now, let's go!"

"*Woof!*" Hank barked and ran out through the bedroom door.

Peter led the way down the long hallway, past the tall wooden library doors, and into the living room in the center of Great-Uncle Solomon's huge house.

He stopped. "Which way?"

Mary pointed to a hallway in the back corner of the room. "I think it's that way."

"You're probably right," said Peter. She was always right.

Peter walked across the living room, past Great-Uncle Solomon's big, comfy reading chair.

"*Woof!*"

Peter turned around. Hank was barking at the shiny suit of armor that stood perfectly still in the hallway leading to the library.

"Come on, Hank," said Peter. "I've told you before that it's not alive." He walked over and tapped on the hollow armor.

Hank didn't move. He just stared at the armor.

"Look!" said Mary. "The sword is gone."

"That's odd," said Peter. "Wait! He's holding

something else." Peter pried open the fingers of the metal glove and found an old iron key shaped like a cross. "What do you think this is for?"

"I don't know," said Mary. "But we should probably take it with us."

Peter nodded and put the key in the adventure bag. He headed to the hallway in the corner of the living room.

At the end of the hallway stood a tall wooden door. It wasn't like the other doors in the house. It was painted red and had an old, rusty doorknob.

"I can't believe we never noticed this door before," said Mary.

"Maybe we weren't ready," said Peter.

Mary raised her eyebrows. "Ready for what?"

Peter reached for the doorknob. "Let's find out." He turned it as hard as he could, but it wouldn't open. "Maybe we aren't ready after all."

"Try the key," said Mary.

"Oh yeah," said Peter. He reached in the adventure bag and pulled out the key. He stuck it in the keyhole and turned.

Click!

Peter swung the door wide open. A spiral staircase led up the stone walls of the tower.

Peter led the way up the stairs—round and round, higher and higher.

At the top, they entered a circular room surrounded by windows. An old wooden box sat on a table in the middle of the room.

"There's not much up here," Peter

said. "I thought there would be something more exciting than just one little box."

"*Woof!*"

Peter heard footsteps coming up the stairs and turned to see Great-Uncle Solomon walking into the room.

Great-Uncle Solomon adjusted his round glasses. "I see you found my greatest archaeological discovery!" He walked over and carefully picked up the small box.

Mary's eyes got as big as church bells. "Why, what's in the box?"

"A cup!" said Great-Uncle Solomon.

"A cup? Why is a cup such a big deal?" said Peter.

"It's not just any cup," said Great-Uncle Solomon. "I believe it might have been the last cup that Jesus used before . . ."

Roar!

The lion's roar echoed through the tower.

Great-Uncle Solomon set the box back on the table. "I'll show you later. Hurry! You don't want to keep the lion waiting." He looked at his pocket watch. "And your parents will be back any minute."

"Let's go!" said Peter.

Hank ran down the stairs. Peter raced after him with Mary close behind. Peter reached the bottom of the spiral stairs and rushed past the suit of armor. He slid to a stop in front of the tall library doors. He reached for the lion's-head handle and turned.

Click!

He swung the door open, and they all ran in.

Roar! The sound came from the bookshelves on the right. Mary quickly found the red book with the lion's head painted in gold on the cover. She pulled it off the shelf.

The bookshelf slid open to reveal the hidden room. It was dark, except for a glowing clay pot in the center of the room that held the scrolls.

Peter and Mary walked into the room and looked into the glowing clay pot.

"There's only one scroll left," said Mary.

Peter picked up the scroll.

"What's on the red wax seal?" said Mary.

Peter squinted. "It looks like a cross."

"Let's see where it takes us!" said Mary.

Peter broke the wax seal holding the scroll together.

Suddenly, the walls shook. Books fell to the floor. Then the library crumbled around them and disappeared.

2

New Friends, Old Enemies

"Baaaa! Baaaa!"

"Woof! Woof!"

Peter looked around. He and Mary were standing in the middle of a wooden pen full of white, fluffy sheep. Hank chased the sheep around in circles.

"Yuck!" said Peter. "What's that smell?" He stepped forward to grab Hank's collar.

Squish!

Mary held her nose. "I think you just stepped in it!"

Peter looked at the bottom of his shoe. "*Ugh*! I found the smell."

"*Woof! Woof!*" Hank kept barking at the sheep.

"What are you kids doing in there?" shouted a large man standing outside the pen. He wore a rough brown robe. "Your dog better not hurt my sheep!"

"Hank, sit!" said Peter.

Hank stopped chasing the sheep and sat down.

"He won't hurt your sheep," said Peter. "I promise."

"He better not," said the man. "They are worth lots of money, but they have to be perfect with no marks or scratches."

"Why?" said Peter.

"So they can be sacrificed at the Temple," said the man. He pointed to the tall, white building with a golden roof next to them.

"*Grrrr!*"

Peter saw a tall Roman soldier coming toward them. He was wearing bronze armor and had bright red feathers on the top of his helmet.

"Is there a problem here?" growled the soldier, reaching for his sword.

"No problem," said Peter.

"Everything is fine," said the man in the brown robe.

The Roman soldier stared into Peter's eyes. "Let's keep it that way."

The man opened the sheep pen. Hank trotted out in front of Peter.

Mary stepped out of the pen. "Thanks for helping us."

"I wasn't helping you," said the man. "I was helping me. Now leave, before you get us all kicked out of the temple courtyard."

"Okay, okay," said Peter. "We won't cause any more problems."

Peter turned around and saw a sea of people in the courtyard. They were buying and selling animals and pushing and shoving each other. It was a big, noisy mess.

"Why are so many people here?" asked Peter.

"I'm not sure," said Mary. "Maybe it's a festival."

"May I pet your dog?" said a small voice behind them.

Peter turned and saw a young girl who looked

a little younger than him. She had dark, curly hair and sparkling eyes.

"Yes," said Mary. "He's very friendly."

The little girl leaned into a wooden crutch and limped toward Hank. Peter noticed her left foot. It was a little twisted in her sandal.

Mary elbowed Peter's ribs.

He didn't mean to stare. He quickly looked back up to the girl's eyes. They weren't quite as sparkly as before.

"His name is Hank," said Peter, trying not to look at the girl's crutch.

The little girl bent down and rubbed Hank's head. "He is beautiful," she said. She stood up straight. "My name is Sarah."

"I'm Peter, and this is my sister, Mary," said Peter.

Hank leaned into Sarah as she petted him.

"He really likes you," said Peter.

Sarah smiled, and her eyes lit up again.

"Sarah! Sarah!" a deep voice broke through the noise of the crowd.

"That's my dad," said Sarah. "I have to go."

A young couple spotted Sarah and rushed over. "There you are!" said the man.

They must be Sarah's parents, thought Peter.

Sarah's mom reached down and hugged her. "We thought we'd lost you."

"Sorry," said Sarah. "I will try to keep up."

Her dad smiled. "I know you will," he said. "Now let's pick our offering and go to the Temple to worship God."

Sarah turned to Peter and Mary. "Would you like to come with us? My parents and I journeyed for a long time to reach Jerusalem and the Temple," she said, "all the way from Cyrene in Africa."

"That is a long way!" said Mary. "We would love to come."

"Get your Passover lamb!" shouted a man next to a sheep pen. "These are the best sheep you will find in all of the temple market!"

"We'll take one," said Sarah's dad. He reached in a dusty pouch and pulled out some coins.

The sheep salesman laughed. "That's not enough money!" he said.

"It is all I have," said Sarah's dad. "We've come a long way, and we need a sacrifice."

The man turned and stepped into the crowded sheep pen. "Well, I might have one for you." He shoved the big, fluffy sheep to the side with his shepherd's staff. "There you are."

Peter looked where the man was pointing. He

saw a small, spotted lamb crouched in the back of the pen.

The man nudged it with his staff. "Get up."

The little lamb slowly stood and limped across the pen. One of its back legs was wobbly. The lamb went through the gate and walked right up to Sarah.

Sarah smiled. "He's just like me."

"He's perfect," said her dad. "We'll take him. How much do we owe you?"

The man grabbed all of the coins in Sarah's dad's hand. "That should be enough!"

"But that's all our money!" said Sarah's mom.

The man shouted, "Now it's all *my* money!"

"You're a thief!" said Peter.

"The lamb is not worth that much," said Sarah's dad.

The man pushed Sarah's dad back with his staff.

"Grrrr!" Hank growled.

"Get out of here before I call a soldier over and tell him you stole the lamb!" said the sheep salesman.

Peter saw Sarah's dad glance over at a soldier who was standing nearby. He looked back at his family. "Okay," he said. "We'll leave."

Sarah looked up at her dad. "It will be okay. He's a good little lamb."

Sarah's dad put his hand on her shoulder and smiled. "You're right. Let's go to the Temple."

Mary and Peter walked beside Sarah as they made their way toward the tall building with the gleaming golden roof. Hank made sure the little lamb stayed with them.

When they reached the stairs leading up to the Temple, Mary whispered, "Peter, look! It's the Pharisees."

Peter looked up the stairs and saw a group of

men wearing
dark robes and
head coverings.
They were looking down at everyone in the
courtyard.

"Up we go," said Sarah's dad, leading the way.

"Where do you think you're going?" said
one of the Pharisees at the top of the stairs. He
stepped in front of Sarah and her parents. He had
a golden staff and was dressed in black from head
to toe.

Peter grabbed Mary's arm and pulled her behind a large pot holding a palm tree.

"What are you doing?" said Mary.

"I think that's the Enemy, Satan," said Peter.

Peter thought about their last adventure. "Remember, he was disguised as a Pharisee the last time we saw him."

Mary peeked around the pot. "That's definitely him."

Peter thought about the last adventure again. Satan had accused Peter and Mary of stealing a scroll from the Temple and had tried to arrest them. And Peter had overheard Satan plotting to get rid of Jesus.

"I bet he's still planning to destroy Jesus and rule the world," said Mary.

"You might be right," said Peter. "We have to find Jesus and the disciples and warn them."

"We'll need to be careful," said Mary. "Satan

knows that we know about his plan, remember? He'll try to keep us from stopping him."

"That's true," said Peter. "Where's Hank?"

Mary pointed. "He's still out there with Sarah. I hope Satan doesn't recognize him."

Peter peered around the pot. Mary poked her head out beneath his.

The Pharisee slammed his golden staff on the stairs. "I asked you a question! Where are you going?"

"We are taking our offering to the Temple," said Sarah's dad.

"We're going to worship God," said Sarah. She stumbled as she stepped forward. The little lamb limped up beside her.

The Pharisee shook his head. "You're not going in with that pitiful little offering."

"What's wrong with him?" said Sarah.

The Pharisee rolled his eyes. "That lamb has

spots, and he limps. God won't accept such a broken offering."

Sarah's shoulders slumped. Peter thought he saw a tear roll down her dusty cheek.

Her father knelt down and wiped her cheek. "It will be okay," he said. "One day the Great King will come and save us from all of this."

The Pharisee slammed his golden staff on the ground again. "There is no Great King coming! We already have a king—King Herod! Now leave!"

"*Grrrr!*" Hank moved in front of Sarah.

"Where did you get that dog?" said the Pharisee. "He looks very familiar."

"He belongs to my new friends," said Sarah, looking around. "They must be around here somewhere."

Peter ducked back behind the pot.

He heard the Pharisee say, "Is it a boy and a girl wearing strange clothes?"

Peter looked down at his shirt. "What's wrong with my clothes?" he whispered. Mary gave him *the look*.

He heard Sarah's voice again. "Yes, do you know them?"

"Yes," said the Pharisee. "We've run into each other a few times."

Peter and Mary froze behind the pot. Peter held his breath.

"Don't worry," said the Pharisee. "I'll find them. And when I do, they'll be sorry they came back."

All of a sudden, a young boy raced into the temple courtyard. The boy pushed into the center of the crowd and started shouting. "The King is coming! The Great King is coming!"

3

THE GREAT KING

"The Great King is coming!" The boy's voice echoed through the courtyard.

"There is no Great King!" shouted the Pharisee with the golden staff. "Soldiers, keep that boy quiet!"

Peter snuck a peek down the stairs and saw several Roman soldiers marching toward the boy.

The boy saw the soldiers and ran to the gates at the end of the courtyard. "The King is coming!" he shouted again.

The crowd gathered around him and blocked the soldiers from getting to him.

"Where is the King?" shouted an older lady. "We've been waiting so long for him to come and save us."

"He's coming down the Mount of Olives!" said the boy. "Follow me!"

Peter looked around the palm tree again and looked back at Sarah and her parents.

Sarah was looking up at her dad. "Can we go and see the King?"

"Yes," her dad said, turning to the Pharisee. "We're not welcome here."

Sarah's dad bent over and picked up the little lamb and Sarah.

Sarah and her family joined the crowd flowing out of the temple courtyard.

Peter whistled. Hank spotted them and ran behind the palm tree. "Stay with us, Hank."

Peter looked around the palm tree again and saw the Pharisees talking in a huddle.

"Let's go," whispered Peter. "The Pharisees aren't looking."

Peter led the way down the stairs and dashed into the crowd. Mary followed, and Hank darted between groups of people. They made it safely to the temple gate.

"Did the Pharisee see us?" said Mary.

Peter looked back into the courtyard. "I'm not sure. He's gone and so are the other Pharisees."

"Well, let's get out of here before he sees us," said Mary.

"Yeah," said Peter. "Let's go see this Great King everyone is so excited about."

Peter, Mary, and Hank followed the crowd through the temple gate. They walked down the cobblestone streets until they reached the wall surrounding the city of Jerusalem.

Peter could feel the excitement in the air. He saw several people cutting branches from palm trees and lining up along the street like they were waiting for a parade.

"Here he comes!" shouted a man.

Men, women, and children waved their palm branches in the air and laid their coats on the road.

"Hosanna!" shouted a woman across the road. "Save us!"

Soon people throughout the crowd were shouting, "Hosanna!"

"Hosanna!" shouted Mary.

Peter jumped. Mary never got very excited, and he couldn't remember ever hearing her shout that loud.

"Sorry," said Mary. "I got a little carried away."

The crowd grew thicker as more and more people showed up to see the King. Several people pushed their way in front of Peter and Mary.

"I can't see," said Mary.

"Ruff! Ruff!" Hank barked and took off.

"Stop, Hank!" said Peter.

But Hank kept going. He weaved his way through the crowd like he was chasing someone.

Peter sighed and took off after Hank. Mary kept pace with him, navigating around the people in their way.

"There he is!" said Mary.

Hank was standing right next to Sarah and her family. She was bent over petting Hank.

Sarah saw them and waved. "Come up here! My dad found a good spot to see the King."

Peter and Mary pushed through the shouting people. They reached Sarah's family just as her mom said, "He's coming!" She pointed down the road.

"Back up!" said a man. "Clear the way!"

"Look!" said Mary. "It's Simon Peter!"

"What's he doing with the King?" said Peter.

"I don't know," said Mary.

Peter waved his arms. "Hey, Simon!"

Simon turned and saw Peter. He smiled and ran over.

"Where have you been?" said Simon. "I haven't seen you in weeks. It was like you three just disappeared after Jesus raised Lazarus from the dead."

"Yeah," said Peter. "It's complicated."

"Well, I am happy to see you again," said Simon.

"We're happy to see you too," said Mary.

"Simon, we have something really important we need to tell you!" said Peter, remembering Satan's plan.

The people shouted louder and waved their palm branches high in the air.

"Bless the King who comes in the name of the Lord!" shouted a man behind Peter.

Simon looked over his shoulder. "You can tell me later! I've got to clear the way." He turned and ran down the road.

"Look, Peter!" said Mary. "There's James and John and the other disciples."

"*Grrrr!*" Hank growled as Judas walked down the road.

Then Mary's jaw dropped. Peter turned to see what she was looking at.

He couldn't believe his eyes. It was Jesus! He was riding a small donkey down the middle of the street.

"Jesus! Jesus!" shouted Peter. He felt the scroll shake in the adventure bag.

Jesus looked at Peter and smiled. "It's good to see you again, Peter! Good to see you, Mary!"

"*Woof!*" Hank barked and wagged his tail.

"Good to see you too, Hank!" said Jesus. He waved as he kept riding the little donkey down the road.

Peter turned and saw Sarah staring at him.

"You know the Great King?" said Sarah.

"Yes," said Peter. A huge smile spread across his face. "His name is Jesus." Peter felt the scroll shake in the bag again. He wanted to take the scroll out, but he knew he couldn't let Sarah see it.

"How do you know him?" said Sarah.

"We met him by the Sea of Galilee," said Mary. "And he's not just a king, he's the Son of God!"

"And he can do miracles," said Peter. "He

raised a man from the dead, and he healed my leg."

Sarah looked down at her crutch.

"Would you like to meet him?" asked Peter.

Sarah nodded really big. "I would love to!"

"Follow me," said Peter.

Peter pushed forward, darting and dodging through the crowd with Mary and Hank on his tail.

"We're almost there!" said Peter. He turned around, but Sarah was gone.

"Oh no!" said Mary. "We must have lost her in the crowd."

"Let's go back and find her," said Peter.

"I think we have bigger problems," said Mary, pointing ahead of them.

A group of Pharisees was standing in the middle of the road blocking Jesus' way.

"This can't be good!" said Peter.

4

TROUBLE AT THE TEMPLE

The Pharisees stood in a line across the road leading to the Temple.

Jesus stopped his donkey. The disciples stood behind him.

The Pharisee stepped forward and pounded his golden staff on the road. "Why is everyone shouting about a King?" He pointed his staff at the palace in the distance. "Herod is our king! This man on this pitiful little donkey is no king!"

"He *should* be our king!" shouted a man in the crowd. "He can do miracles!"

The people cheered.

"He heals people!" shouted a lady.

"Lies!" shouted the Pharisee. "It's all lies!"

Peter's heart pounded. "He healed me!"

Mary spun toward Peter and gave him *the look*.

The Pharisee turned and stared at Peter with his cold, dark eyes. "Well, look who's here," he snarled. "What did you say?"

"Jesus healed me," said Peter. "It's true." Peter felt the scroll shake. He gripped the bag under his arm.

The Pharisee slowly shook his head and walked toward them.

"Woof! Woof!" Hank barked and ran in front of Peter and Mary.

The Pharisee stopped. He looked around at the crowd and at Jesus.

"I'll deal with you meddling kids and your nasty dog later," he said. "I have bigger issues right now."

"Hosanna!" shouted someone in the crowd. "Bless the King who comes in the name of the Lord!"

The Pharisee gritted his teeth and turned to Jesus. "Tell them to be quiet!"

Jesus looked at the cheering crowd. "If they are quiet, the rocks will shout out in praise instead!"

The crowd cheered louder as Jesus and the disciples walked past the Pharisees. The sun began to set behind the Temple. It cast a long shadow across the road.

Peter glanced at Mary. She nodded, and they chased after Jesus, staying as close behind him as they could. Peter quickly pulled Mary into the crowd as they passed the Pharisees. He heard them talking and stopped.

"Everyone is following him. Some are even calling him the King of the Jews," Peter heard one of the Pharisees say. "What are we going to do?"

"We have to destroy him," said the Pharisee with the golden staff, "so we can keep our power over these people."

Peter rushed to catch up to Mary and Hank.

"You were right," said Peter. "Satan is still planning to destroy Jesus. I just heard him talking about it."

"I knew it," said Mary. "Did he see you?"

Peter looked back. "I don't think so. Now he's whispering in someone's ear."

"Who is it?" said Mary.

Peter squinted. "It looks a little bit like Judas, but I can't tell because he's in the shadows."

"There you are!" said a loud voice.

Peter spun around to find Simon Peter. Simon reached down and gave Peter and Mary big hugs. Then he rubbed Hank's head.

Peter looked back at the Pharisee, but the mysterious man was gone.

"There's something we need to tell you," said Peter.

"What is it?" said Simon, leaning down.

"Grrrr!"

Judas appeared behind Simon. "It's time to go. Jesus is waiting."

"You can tell me later, Peter," Simon said. "Where are you three staying?"

Peter shrugged. "We don't have any plans."

"Come with us," said Simon. "You can stay at

Lazarus's house. There's lots of room. Isn't there, Judas?"

Judas rolled his eyes. "I don't think Jesus wants kids and a dog hanging around."

"What are you talking about," said Simon. "Jesus loves kids!"

"*Woof!*"

"And dogs!" said Simon. "Now come with us."

Judas gave Peter and Mary a suspicious look as they walked by him. Hank gave a low growl.

"I don't trust him," whispered Peter.

"Me either," said Mary.

Peter talked with Simon Peter, and Mary spoke with some of the other disciples as they all walked with Jesus out of Jerusalem, over the Mount of Olives, all the way to Lazarus's house.

Peter stopped and looked at the house. It was tall with a row of windows across the second floor. It was big, just like Simon had said. Jesus and the disciples entered the house, and Peter, Mary, and Hank brought up the rear.

Lazarus greeted them as they came in the door. "Come in! Come in! Jesus told me you need a place to stay."

"Yes," said Mary. "We've come on a long journey."

"Come right this way," said Lazarus. "I have the perfect room."

They followed him down a long hallway with colorful carpets. Lazarus opened a door to a room filled with fluffy pillows and sleeping mats.

"This will be perfect," said Mary. "Thank you."

"We will rise early in the morning," said Lazarus. "So get some rest."

"Good night!" said Peter, as Lazarus shut the door.

Peter tossed his adventure bag on a pillow then plopped down on another. He leaned back and sank into the pillow. "I could get used to this."

Hank curled up on a pillow under a large window. A light breeze blew the curtains.

"Grrrr!" Hank stared at the window.

"What is it?" said Mary.

Peter's heart pounded. "I hope it's not Satan."

A big gust of wind blew the curtains wide open.

Peter backed away from the window. Then Michael the angel flew into the room with his mighty wings spread wide.

Peter took a deep breath. "You scared us. We thought you were Satan."

"Where have you been?" said Mary. "We were worried he would catch us!"

"The Enemy, Satan, has been very busy with his plan," said Michael.

"I know," said Peter. "We need to tell Jesus and the disciples about his plan to destroy Jesus and rule the world!"

The scroll shook in the adventure bag. Peter pulled it out and started to unroll it.

"Wait," said Michael. "Don't open it until we go over the rules of the adventure."

Peter sighed. He didn't like waiting, and he didn't like rules.

Michael held up one finger. "First rule: You

have to solve the secret of the scroll in eight days or you will be stuck here."

"We have to solve it," said Mary. "Our parents are almost back from their trip."

Peter put his hand on Mary's shoulder. "We can solve it. We've done it before, and we can do it again!"

Mary nodded. "You're right. We can do it."

Michael held up two fingers. "Second rule: you can't tell anyone where you are from or that you're from the future."

Peter nodded and so did Mary.

Michael held up three fingers. "Third rule: you can't try to change the past."

"Does that mean we can't tell Jesus and the disciples about the Enemy's plan?" said Mary.

The scroll shook again.

"That's right," said Michael, "You will have to trust God to carry out his own plan."

Peter was worried about Satan's plan. But he remembered all the times God had come through for him in their previous adventures. He would have to trust God.

Peter and Mary nodded their heads in agreement.

"Now you can open the scroll," said Michael.

Peter unrolled the scroll and saw nine words written in strange letters. The first word glowed

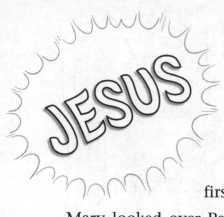

and transformed into the word: JESUS.

"We did it!" said Peter. "We solved the first word."

Mary looked over Peter's shoulder. "That's a lot of words to solve. And it's written in Greek. This isn't going to be easy."

"We'll work together," said Peter.

"He's right," said Michael. "Now get some sleep. You have a big adventure ahead of you."

Peter nodded. "We have to watch out for the Enemy."

"Yes," said Michael, "and remember that he can influence other people to help with his plan."

"Like who?" said Peter.

"I can't tell you," said Michael. "Trust God to show you the truth."

"Can you give us a hint?" said Mary.

"No," said Michael. "I must go for now." He spread his wings and flew out of the window like a bolt of lightning.

Peter rested his head on a fluffy pillow. Hank curled up on a pillow next to him. Peter closed his eyes. He was nervous, but he couldn't wait to see what was going to happen next.

5

Not in My Father's House

"Rise and shine!"

Peter heard Lazarus's voice through the bedroom door. Peter got up from the big pillow and stretched. His stomach rumbled. "I'm hungry!"

Mary yawned. "You're always hungry."

Hank ran over and stood at the door.

"It looks like Hank is hungry too," said Mary.

Peter opened the door, and the smell of

fresh-baked bread filled the air. Hank stuck his nose high in the air and sniffed. His tail started wagging.

Peter grabbed the adventure bag and headed out the door.

"Where are you going?" said Mary.

"Wherever my nose takes me," said Peter.

He ran down the long hallway with Mary close behind. He rounded the corner and found a large room. Jesus and the disciples were sitting around a table.

"Good morning!" said Jesus. "Have a seat. We're about to eat."

"There's room over here," said Simon.

"Thanks," said Peter. He plopped down on a pillow beside Simon. Mary sat down on Simon's other side. Hank settled on a pillow behind them.

"What were you trying to tell me in Jerusalem?" asked Simon. "It sounded important."

"Oh yeah," said Peter. "It's about the Pharisee with the golden—*ouch*!"

Mary kicked him under the table. She gave him *the look*, and Peter remembered that he couldn't tell.

"Are you okay?" said Simon.

"Yes," said Peter. "I'm just a little hungry."

"So, what were you going to tell me about the Pharisee?" Simon said.

"We really can't tell you," said Mary. "It's a secret."

Simon laughed. "You kids are full of secrets."

Just then a young lady came into the room and sat down next to Jesus. "It's good to see you, Mary," said Jesus. "Where is Martha?"

"I don't know," Mary said. "I'm sure my sister is busy doing something."

Martha rushed into the room with a large basket full of food. She gave her sister an upset look. "I've been busy making breakfast for everyone!"

"I would have helped," said her sister.

Martha rolled her eyes as she put the food on the table.

"Breakfast looks amazing, Martha!" said Jesus. "Thank you."

Peter's stomach growled when he saw the basket filled with bread, cheese, and fruit. Jesus said a prayer to bless the food, and everyone filled their plates and bellies.

"Where are we going today?" said Simon.

"Back to Jerusalem," said Jesus.

"The people want to make you king," said Judas. He banged his fist on the table. "The time has come for us to take power and take over the palace!"

"The Kingdom of God is not about palaces," said Jesus. "It's about people." He looked over at Peter and Mary. "It's about God being with his people."

Judas didn't look happy with Jesus.

"Where are we going in Jerusalem?" said Thomas.

"We're going to the Temple," said Jesus, "so I can be with the people."

Everyone helped clean up, then they left for Jerusalem. Peter threw sticks for Hank as they made the long walk back over the Mount of Olives, through the valley, and through the tall walls surrounding Jerusalem.

Finally, Peter saw the temple gate ahead of him. He walked into the crowded courtyard behind Mary and the rest of the group.

Jesus moved through the noisy crowd toward the center of the courtyard. The sound of sheep baaaaing and birds tweeting filled the air.

"Gross," said Peter. "These animals stink!"

"Get your sheep here!" shouted a salesman. "They're the best sheep in the Temple!"

"No!" shouted another salesman. "Buy my sheep! They're perfect!"

"*Grrrr!*" Hank growled at one of the sheep salesmen.

"There's the man who stole money from Sarah's dad," said Peter.

"Get out of here, kid!" the man said. "Before I call the soldiers."

"But you're stealing from these people!" said Mary.

"So what!" said the man. "Nobody's going to stop me."

Jesus shook his head and anger filled his eyes. "What has happened to my Father's house? It's not supposed to be this way!" said Jesus. "My Father's house should be a place of prayer." He looked at the chaos around him. "Leave! All of you thieves, leave!"

Jesus opened the sheep pen. The sheep ran out. He pushed over tables. Coins clanged and rolled across the courtyard.

The man dropped to his knees and scooped up the money. He ran out of the courtyard, trying to catch his sheep.

Peter stood next to Mary and watched as Jesus opened another pen and another. Sheep were running everywhere. The soldiers and the salesmen tried to catch them, but there were just too many. Hank raced around, trying to herd the sheep out of the courtyard. Then Jesus started opening the bird cages. Doves and pigeons filled the air. Mary ducked as they swooped over her.

"Stop!" shouted someone from the top of the temple steps.

But Jesus didn't stop until all of the thieves,

sheep, and birds were gone. Peace and quiet filled the courtyard.

Peter looked up the stairs and saw the Pharisee with the golden staff standing with the other Pharisees and priests in front of the Temple.

"What have you done?" said the Pharisee. He pointed at the people still standing in the courtyard. "How are all these pitiful sinners going to make God happy without sacrifices?" he said. "Sacrifices are the way to God. There is no other way!"

Jesus looked up at the Temple. "God's house should be a house of prayer! But you have made it a place for thieves!"

Peter saw anger in the faces of the Pharisees and priests.

Someone tapped Peter on the shoulder.

6

THE PLOT UNFOLDS

Peter turned around. Sarah stood behind him with the little, spotted lamb by her side.

Peter remembered the promise he had made to Sarah. He walked over to Jesus. "Excuse me, Jesus. This is our friend, Sarah."

Sarah hobbled closer to Jesus and knelt down in front of him.

Jesus knelt too. He looked into Sarah's eyes and smiled. She smiled back.

"It's nice to meet you," said Jesus. "What a beautiful lamb you have. It looks like you are taking great care of him."

Sarah pointed to her parents. "My mom and dad are helping me."

"I can tell you all are doing a good job," said Jesus. "Is there something I can help you with?"

Sarah looked down at her little, wooden crutch. "Can you help me walk?"

Jesus looked into Sarah's eyes. "Do you believe I can heal you?"

Sarah nodded her head. "Yes, I believe."

Jesus stood up, took five steps back, and held out his arms. "Come to me."

Peter held his breath.

Sarah stood up. She wiggled her toes. She dropped her crutch. She took one step—then another.

"She's walking!" cried Mary.

A smile filled Sarah's face, and she ran to Jesus and gave him a big hug.

Sarah turned to her mom
and dad. "I can walk!" She
spun in a circle. "And I
can dance!"

Sarah's dad grabbed
her hands. They danced
like no one else was
there. Peter grinned
and looked at Mary.
She was smiling too.

Then Sarah's dad turned to Jesus. A tear ran
down his cheek. "Thank you!"

The people in the courtyard cheered.

"Hosanna!" shouted a young boy.

"Save us, Great King!" shouted a little girl.

The Pharisees and priests walked down the
temple steps.

Peter and Mary moved back into the crowd.

"Make them be quiet!" said one of the priests.

"Don't you hear what they are saying?"

"Yes," said Jesus. "Haven't you read in the scrolls that out of the mouth of the young, God will be praised?"

The children clapped and praised God. Their parents joined them, and a joyful sound filled the temple courtyard.

Peter peeked through the crowd. The Pharisee was shaking his head and squeezing the golden staff.

"The Pharisees and priests aren't happy," Peter said to Mary. "I think they're mad because Jesus is making a new way to God."

Mary rubbed her chin. "Maybe Jesus is the way to God."

Peter felt the bag move under his arm. "The scroll is shaking."

"Let's go see what it says," said Mary.

Peter weaved through the crowd and stopped behind a tall column on the edge of the courtyard. When Mary caught up, he unrolled the scroll. The second, third, and fourth words glowed and transformed into: IS THE WAY.

Peter read out loud, "Jesus is the way." He gave Mary a high-five.

"*Grrrr!*" Hank growled at something on the other side of the column.

Peter looked around the column. "It's the Pharisees and priests," he whispered. "They're coming this way."

He quickly tucked the scroll back into the adventure bag.

"What should we do?" whispered Mary.

Peter put his arm around Hank. "Be still and very quiet."

Peter heard the voice of the Pharisee with the

golden staff. "We must destroy Jesus! Everyone is listening to him instead of us."

"He's right over there," said another voice. "Let's get him now."

"Not yet," said the Pharisee. "There are too many people around him."

"What do you suggest?" said another Pharisee.

"We need someone on the inside to help us," said the Pharisee. "Someone close to Jesus."

"Who would turn against Jesus?" said a priest.

"I know the perfect person," said the Pharisee. "Let's go tell the High Priest the plan."

Peter heard them walk away. He looked around the column. They were gone.

"I wonder who the Pharisee was talking about," said Peter. "Who would betray Jesus?"

Mary scratched her head. "I think I might know. But I need more evidence."

"I'll keep my eyes open," said Peter.

The sun began to set behind the Temple. "It's getting late," said Peter. "Let's find Jesus and the disciples."

Peter and Mary found Jesus and the disciples at the temple gate. They headed back to Lazarus's house together. Along the way, Peter listened to the disciples. He wondered if one of them might turn against Jesus and help the Enemy.

When they reached the house, everyone was tired and quiet from the long day. Peter joined Mary as she headed to their room. Hank fell asleep as soon as he laid down. Peter fell asleep a few minutes later.

They all spent the next day back at the Temple. Peter was surprised by how different it was. The thieves were gone, along with their noisy sheep and birds. Jesus really did make a difference.

That night, Peter pulled out the adventure journal. He sat by the window in his room and wrote about all the things he had seen and heard.

Day 3

Jesus spent the day teaching and healing at the Temple. He healed one lady that was blind. She was so happy. She kept talking about how beautiful everything was. She said Hank was the most beautiful creature she had ever seen. I think Hank was a little embarrassed. More and more people came to the Temple to meet Jesus. He taught them

to love God with all their hearts, minds, and strength. He also said it is very important to love

your neighbor. Everyone listened quietly to
Jesus—except for the priests and Pharisees.
They kept interrupting him and asking a
bunch of questions. They were so rude. I
can't wait to see what Jesus does tomorrow.

Peter put the journal away. Mary and Hank
were both snoring. He covered his ears and went
to sleep.

7

Out of the Shadows

The next morning, Peter and Mary joined Jesus and the disciples for breakfast. Martha kept bringing more and more food.

Peter rubbed his full belly. "I could get used to this."

"Are we going back to the Temple today?" asked Thomas.

"No," said Jesus. "We are going to a friend's house. He's having a party for me."

Peter loved parties. He ran to the bedroom and grabbed the adventure bag. "Come on, Mary!"

he said, as he ran to catch up with Jesus and the disciples. They walked down a long dusty road until they came to a house. Jesus knocked on the door.

"Thank you for coming!" said a man with a long white beard.

Peter recognized the man. Jesus had healed him at the Temple.

"It's good to see you," said Jesus.

"Come in! Come in!" said the man. He led them into a big room with a few pillows scattered around. "Have a seat."

"Thank you for inviting us," said Jesus.

Knock! Knock!

The man opened the door. "More guests! Come in!" He tossed more pillows on the floor as the guests entered.

This went on for the rest of the day—more knocking, more guests, and more pillows.

Everyone was coming to be with Jesus. Peter watched as Jesus laughed and talked with everyone.

Later that day, Peter noticed Lazarus's sister Mary walking through the room with a fancy, sparkling jar. She set it on the table in front of Jesus. Then she broke the top off the jar and poured something out on Jesus' head and feet.

"What is she doing?" asked Peter.

Hank stuck his nose in the air and sniffed. He started wagging his tail. So Peter stuck his nose in the air and took a big sniff. Whatever was in the

bottle smelled amazing—like flowers and cinnamon and cotton candy all mixed together.

"*Achoo!*" Mary sneezed. "I don't know what that is, but I think I'm allergic to it."

"What a waste!" shouted Judas. "She could have sold that expensive perfume and given the money to the poor."

Peter looked at Lazarus's sister. Her shoulders slumped and she stared at the floor.

Jesus stood beside her and looked across the room at Judas. "Leave her alone. She has done a beautiful thing for me."

She lifted her head back up. A smile filled her face.

Judas scowled and stormed out of the house.

"Let's follow him," said Peter.

"I don't know," said Mary. "He looks pretty upset."

"But what if he's the one the Pharisee was

talking about?" whispered Peter. "The one who is going to betray Jesus."

"You're right," said Mary. "Let's hurry before he gets away."

They snuck through the crowd and slipped out the door without anyone noticing.

Mary looked around. "Where did he go?"

Hank sniffed the air and took off down the dusty road. Peter raced after Hank, and Mary raced after Peter.

The sun was setting. Peter couldn't see very far ahead. Hank finally stopped at the bottom of the Mount of Olives.

Peter squinted and looked up the side of the rocky mountain. He saw someone walking into a clump of trees at the top.

"Is that Judas?" said Peter.

"It's hard to tell," said Mary. "It's getting so dark."

"Let's go see," said Peter. "Maybe we'll find a clue that will help us solve another word."

"That's true," said Mary. "Okay, let's go."

Mary led the way up the mountain. Peter climbed as quietly as he could, sneaking from olive tree to olive tree behind Mary and Hank. Finally, they made it to the top.

"There's Judas," whispered Mary.

They hid behind some bushes. Peter saw Judas standing in the middle of the trees, looking around.

"Judas," a deep voice came from behind one of the trees.

There was a figure standing in the shadows.

"I knew you would come," said the voice.

"Who is that?" said Mary.

The man took another step out of the shadows. The moonlight reflected off his golden staff.

"It's Satan," whispered Peter.

"Judas, I have some friends I would like you to meet," said the Pharisee. "Come on out."

Peter saw several men wearing colorful robes and head coverings. He recognized the priests from the Temple.

"This is Judas," said the Pharisee. "He will bring Jesus to you."

"Do you have my money?" said Judas.

A priest tossed a small bag to Judas. Judas opened the bag and counted out thirty pieces of silver.

"I'll do it," said Judas.

"When?" said one of the priests.

"Soon," said Judas. "Very soon."

"I knew it was Judas who would betray Jesus!" whispered Peter.

"Shhhh," said Mary.

"What was that?" said Judas.

8

A FEAST FOR A KING

Peter's heart pounded in his chest. He moved further back behind the bush.

"I heard a noise," said Judas.

Peter didn't move a muscle. Mary froze beside him.

"It came from over there," said the Pharisee with the golden staff. "Behind those bushes."

Peter heard footsteps and the snapping of fallen twigs.

"Let's get out of here!" whispered Mary.

Peter popped up from behind the bushes and

stared into the Pharisee's cold, dark eyes. "Run!" shouted Peter.

Mary turned and sprinted away. Peter fled after her.

"You can run, but you can't hide!" shouted the Pharisee. "You can't stop my plan!"

They ran down the mountain and didn't look back. Hank led the way—running and jumping from rock to rock. Peter went as fast as his feet could carry him. Mary was close behind. Peter slid to a stop at the bottom of the mountain. Mary skidded down a second later.

Peter leaned over and took a deep breath. "I can't believe how fast we ran."

"Gravity helped," puffed Mary. "I was just trying not to fall."

Peter looked up the mountain. "I think we got away!"

"Hurry!" said Mary. "Let's get to Lazarus's house before they catch us."

The house was dark and quiet when they got back. They tiptoed to their room. Peter fell asleep quickly. It wasn't hard after all that running.

The next morning, the disciples were already eating when Peter and Mary entered the dining area. Peter yawned and took a seat. Judas came in last and sat next to him. Peter wondered if Judas had seen them on the mountain.

"Hey, Judas," said Simon. "Where did you disappear to last night?"

"I had some business to take care of," grunted Judas.

Simon looked over at Peter, Mary, and Hank.

"And where did you three go? You didn't get back till after dark."

Peter gulped. He wanted to tell Simon, but he knew he couldn't. "We went for a long walk."

Judas shifted his eyes toward Peter. "Kids shouldn't be out at night. It can be dangerous."

The room grew quiet. Peter felt awkward.

Jesus broke the silence. "It's Passover. Simon and John, I need you to go and prepare the Passover meal for us."

"Where should we go?" said Simon.

"Go to Jerusalem," said Jesus. "You will see a man carrying a large jar of water. Follow him to a house."

"Then what?" said Simon.

"Tell the owner of the house that I sent you and want to celebrate Passover with my disciples," said Jesus.

Simon and John stood up from the table.

Peter glanced over at Judas. Judas was staring at him with suspicious eyes.

"Can we go with you?" blurted out Peter.

"Sure," said Simon. "We can use the help."

Peter grabbed the adventure bag and put it over his shoulder.

Judas grabbed Peter's arm and pulled him close. "I know you were on the mountain last night," he whispered. "You better not tell anyone."

"Are you coming?" said Simon.

Peter pulled his arm away. "Yes, I'm coming."

Peter couldn't leave the house fast enough. He joined Mary, Simon, and John outside.

Jerusalem was busy when they arrived. Lots of people filled the streets. They carried baskets full of vegetables, bread, and herbs.

"How are we supposed to find a man carrying a jar of water?" said Simon. "There are so many people."

Hank barked and ran through the crowd.

"Hank will find him," said Mary. "He's good at finding things."

"Yeah," said Peter. "He's the world's smartest dog!"

"Might as well," said John. "We're not doing a very good job of finding him ourselves."

They squeezed through the crowd after Hank.

"I see Hank!" said Peter. "He's right behind a man carrying a jar."

The man started walking faster and faster. Hank stayed right behind him.

"Wait!" shouted Simon.

The man looked over his shoulder, but he didn't stop. He walked even faster through the crowd. Hank sped up, and Peter ran to keep up with him. He glanced back and saw Simon, John, and Mary struggling to keep up. Then the man turned down a side street, ducked into a house, and shut the door.

Peter waited for the others. "This must be the house," said John.

Simon knocked on the door. Peter didn't recognize the man who opened the door. He had a long, curly beard. The man with the jar stood behind him.

"That's them," said the man with the jar. "Those are the ones who were chasing me."

"Calm down," said the man with the beard. He looked back at Simon. "What can I do for you?"

Simon told him Jesus had sent them.

The man smiled. "I've been expecting you. Come with me. I have the perfect place."

Simon led the way as they followed the man

through his house and up some stairs. The man opened a door. Peter walked in and saw a large room with a long table in the middle.

"Thank you," said Simon. The man nodded and left the room. Simon said, "Let's get to work."

Peter placed pillows on the floor around the table, while Mary put plates out. John roasted a lamb over the fire. Simon placed a bowl in the middle of the table.

John passed Mary a platter of flat bread. Peter thought the bread looked like big crackers.

"This reminds me of what Moses did in Egypt," said Peter.

Once again, Mary gave Peter *the look*.

Peter panicked. "I mean . . . isn't this what Moses did before God freed the Israelites from slavery in Egypt?"

"You know a lot about history," said Simon. "Mary, you should listen to your brother."

Peter grinned. "Yeah, I could teach you a thing or two."

Mary rolled her eyes.

"Hey, Peter," said John. "Can you put the last cup in the middle of the table? It's very important."

"Sure," said Peter. "I'll take good care of it."

On his way to the table with the cup, Peter tripped over a pillow. He lost his grip on the cup. It slipped from his fingers, rolled across the table, and fell on the floor.

Peter scrambled across the floor and picked up the cup. As he wiped it off, a small chip of clay broke off the bottom. He set the cup on the table quickly. He looked over at Mary. She just shook her head.

"I think it will still work," Peter said to Simon.

"Let's make sure," said Simon. He slowly poured something into the cup.

Peter held his breath as he watched. Nothing leaked out. He exhaled. "I told you it would work."

Simon stood back and looked around the room. "Everything is ready. Let's go get Jesus and the other disciples."

9

In the Dark of Night

Peter watched the sun set through the window as he sat at the table with Jesus and the disciples to celebrate Passover.

Jesus lit a candle. He looked around the table. "One of you is going to betray me."

The disciples gasped and looked at each other.

"It's not me," said Thomas.

"It's not me either," said John.

Peter looked over at Judas. Judas wasn't looking at the other disciples.

"Who is it?" asked Simon.

Jesus picked up a piece of bread and handed it to Judas. They dipped pieces of bread in the bowl together.

"The one who is going to betray me is the one dipping the bread in the bowl with me," said Jesus.

Judas pulled his hand back from the bowl.

"Go," Jesus said, "and do it quickly."

Judas nervously looked around the table. Then he ran out into the dark night. The disciples

whispered to each other. Peter wondered what would happen next.

Jesus picked up the bread from the middle of the table. He thanked God and broke the bread. Then he said to the disciples, "This is my body, broken for you." He handed a small piece to everyone. They ate it. "Do this to remember me."

Then Jesus picked up the cup in the middle of the table. Peter hoped Jesus wouldn't notice the chip on the bottom.

Jesus held up the cup and thanked God again. "This is my blood. It is poured out for the

forgiveness of sins." Jesus passed the cup around the table.

The meal ended and the disciples stood up. They sang a song that Peter didn't know.

After the song was finished, Jesus invited everyone to come with him. He led the way out of Jerusalem to the Mount of Olives.

Jesus stopped. He turned to his disciples. "Tonight, you will all leave me."

"No," said Simon. "I will never leave you!"

Jesus stepped toward Simon. Peter thought Jesus looked sad. "Tonight, before the rooster crows, you will deny me three times."

"No," said Simon. "I will never deny you!"

All the other disciples agreed.

Jesus turned and walked higher up the mountain. Peter struggled through the darkness after the disciples. His legs were starting to ache. Mary was moving as slowly as he was. They got to the top and went through olive trees to a small garden.

"Sit here while I go to pray," said Jesus to the disciples.

The disciples sat down. Hank sat too.

Jesus took Simon, James, and John with him and walked further into the garden.

Peter leaned over to Mary. "Let's go with them."

"I'm not sure," said Mary. "Jesus didn't ask us to come."

"What if we miss a clue to solve the scroll?" said Peter.

Mary thought for a second. "Okay. But we have to be quiet."

"Come on, Hank," whispered Peter. They walked into the garden.

Mary found a good hiding tree. Peter scrunched up next to her and listened.

"My heart is heavy," said Jesus. "Stay here and pray with me."

Peter saw Simon, James, and John sit down and lean against a tree. They looked very tired.

Jesus took a few steps away and fell to the ground. He cried out, "Father, please don't make me do this! But I will do what you want me to do."

The dark sky was silent.

Jesus cried out again, "Father, please don't make me go through this!"

Peter squinted through the darkness. He saw

sweat dripping from Jesus as he prayed. A breeze blew, and the branches on the trees began to sway. An angel landed beside Jesus.

Peter recognized the angel—it was Michael. He didn't say a word. He just spread his mighty wings around Jesus as he cried out to God. Then Michael flew off into the darkness.

"Father, I will do as you want," said Jesus. He slowly stood to his feet and went back to the disciples. Peter could see them sleeping under the tree. He couldn't believe they could fall asleep at a time like this.

"Wake up," said Jesus. "My betrayer is here."

Simon, James, and John stood and brushed off their robes.

Peter heard a noise coming from the other side of the garden.

"Peter, look!" Mary whispered.

A crowd was walking into the garden carrying

fiery torches, swords, and wooden clubs. Peter recognized some priests and Pharisees surrounded by an angry mob.

Jesus took a few steps forward and stood in front of the mob.

Someone stepped to the front of the crowd. It was Judas. He stood face-to-face with Jesus.

"Hello, teacher," said Judas.

The Pharisee with the golden staff stepped forward and shouted, "Arrest that man!"

The crowd moved toward Jesus with their swords and clubs.

"Grrrr." Hank let out a low growl and moved in front of Peter and Mary. Peter grabbed Mary's hand.

Simon shouted and pulled a sword from his robe. He ran past Peter into the middle of the mob and started swinging. His sword struck the side of one man's head.

The man cried out and fell to his knees. Peter saw blood where one of the man's ears should have been.

"Stop!" said Jesus. He turned to Simon. "Put your sword away. If you live by the sword, you will die by the sword."

Jesus knelt in front of the man. He reached out and touched the man's injured ear. The man stood up and felt his head. Peter inhaled sharply. The man's ear was healed.

Jesus dropped his hands to sides.

The mob pushed Peter and Mary to the side as they surrounded Jesus and wrapped his arms in chains.

Hank barked. Peter watched as Simon and the other disciples ran away into the dark night.

10

THE ROOSTER'S CROW

Peter's heart pounded when he saw Jesus standing in chains. He couldn't believe the disciples had left Jesus when he needed them most.

The mob led Jesus down the mountain toward Jerusalem.

Peter looked at Mary. Her eyes were red, and she looked like she was about to cry. Hank whined and leaned against Mary's leg.

Peter took a deep breath. "I can't believe that just happened. What do we do now?"

"I don't know," said Mary. "We need to solve the scroll, but this is getting dangerous!"

Peter reached into the adventure bag, pulled out the scroll, and read, "Jesus is the Way, __ __, __ __ __." He looked at Mary. "I guess we need to keep following Jesus."

Mary nodded her head. "And keep trusting God."

Peter put the scroll away. "Let's keep going."

Peter led the way as they followed the mob's torches into Jerusalem, past the Temple, and down a side street. Finally, the mob stopped at a big house with a courtyard in front.

Peter saw a group of temple guards and Pharisees warming themselves by a fire in the middle of the courtyard. They laughed and pointed as the mob led Jesus by them in chains.

"They're ready for you!" snarled one of the guards.

The mob pushed Jesus through the large front door of the house.

"*Grrrr.*" Hank growled at the guards as they walked past the fire.

"*Shhhh,*" said Peter. "We don't want anyone to notice us."

Mary snuck through the front door. Peter ducked in after her. In the dim light, Peter saw a room full of priests, Pharisees, and temple guards. Peter slid into a corner of the room and pulled Mary after him.

Peter spotted Jesus. He was standing silently in front of a row of Priests.

Mary pointed to the door. "Look, it's John and Simon."

John made it into the room, but a girl stopped Simon.

"Aren't you one of Jesus' disciples?" she said.

Simon slowly backed up. "No! I don't know him!" He turned and walked out.

"What is he talking about?" said Peter. "Jesus is his best friend."

One of the priests in a fancy robe stepped forward and silenced the crowd.

"Oh no," whispered Mary. "Peter, look who's here."

Peter saw the Pharisee with the golden staff sneaking through the crowd, whispering in people's ears.

"Does anyone have anything to say against this man?" asked a priest.

It reminded Peter of courtroom scenes he had seen on TV, when someone was on trial. He listened as the crowd said terrible things about Jesus.

"They're telling lies," said Peter. "Why won't Jesus defend himself?"

Mary shook her head. "I don't know."

An older priest with a long gray beard quieted the crowd. It was the High Priest Caiaphas. Peter recognized him from their last adventure. The High Priest walked over and stood face-to-face with Jesus. "Tell us if you are the Christ! The Son of God!"

"I am!" Jesus said.

"You can't say that! It's blasphemy!" shouted the High Priest. "You must die!"

The crowd cheered.

"Take him to the Roman governor, Pilate!" said the High Priest. "He will be the judge!"

The temple guards surrounded Jesus. They started pushing and hitting him.

One of the guards covered Jesus' eyes. "Tell us, Great King! Who hit you?"

Mary turned her head. "I can't take it anymore!" She ran out the door.

Peter and Hank raced after her into the courtyard.

"Look," said Peter when he had found Mary. "There's Simon over by the fire."

Peter started to walk over to Simon. Simon looked up and made eye contact with him. Then he turned his back to Peter and Mary. He stared into the fire like he'd never met them before. Peter's stomach twisted. He looked at Mary in disbelief.

A girl pointed across the fire at Simon. "Aren't you one of Jesus' disciples?"

Simon pulled the hood of his robe over the top of his head. "No," he mumbled. "I don't know him."

"You are one of them!" said a man beside him. "I can tell by the way you talk."

"*Ruff!*"

Peter turned to see what Hank was barking at. The sun was beginning to rise above the roof. Peter saw Jesus being pushed out of the door.

"I don't know what you are talking about!" shouted Simon. "I don't know him!"

Cock-a-doodle-doo! Peter heard a rooster crow in the distance.

Peter watched Simon look up from the fire. Jesus was standing there in chains. Simon dropped his head into his hands and wept. Then he ran out of the courtyard.

11

WHAT IS TRUTH?

The sun rose over Jerusalem. The guards, priests, and Pharisees led Jesus out of the courtyard and onto the road. Peter, Mary, and Hank followed the crowd.

The crowd stopped at the bottom of stone steps leading up to a huge stone fortress. The Pharisee banged his golden staff on the ground and shouted for Pilate to come out.

Suddenly, Peter saw a tall man walk out wearing a white robe. He stood at the top of the steps. The man was surrounded by Roman

soldiers dressed in red and covered in bronze armor. They carried shields, and sharp swords hung by their sides.

Pilate looked across the crowd. His eyes stopped on Jesus, who was standing silently in chains. Pilate raised his hand. The crowd fell quiet.

"What are your charges against this man?" shouted Pilate.

The High Priest stepped forward. "He has done evil things. And he says he is the Son of God!" he shouted.

The crowd started shouting again. A row of Roman soldiers held up their shields and took a few steps down the stairs.

Pilate held up his hand, and they stopped. "Bring him to me."

Two of the soldiers marched down the stairs and grabbed Jesus' chains. They led him up to Pilate.

"Come on," said Peter. "Let's try to get closer."

Peter led the way around the crowd toward the edge of the stairs. He pointed to a column. He crouched behind it. Mary snuck over with Hank and joined him.

"Are you a king?" Pilate asked Jesus.

"My kingdom is not an earthly kingdom," said Jesus. "If it was, my followers would have fought for me."

"So, you are a king?" said Pilate.

"You say so yourself," said Jesus. "I have come into the world to speak the Truth. Everyone who loves the Truth listens to me."

"Your own people and priests have handed you over to me," said Pilate. "You speak of truth, but they have accused you of being a liar."

Peter whispered, "Why doesn't Pilate believe him? Jesus is telling the truth. He is the Great King and the Son of God."

Peter felt the scroll shaking in the adventure bag. He pulled it out and unrolled it. Two words glowed and transformed into: THE TRUTH.

Peter quietly read, "Jesus is the Way, the Truth, ___ ___ ___."

Mary looked over his shoulder at the scroll.

"We only have three words left."

"*Shhhh,*" said Peter. He glanced back at Pilate and Jesus.

Pilate led Jesus back to the top of the stairs.

"I find no guilt in this man!" shouted Pilate.

The crowd shouted angrily and shook their fists at Jesus.

Pilate held his hand up again. "Passover tradition says that I can release a prisoner."

Pilate motioned. Soldiers brought out a rough-looking man in a tattered robe. "Do you want me to release this criminal, Barabbas? Or do you want me to release Jesus, the so-called King of the Jews?"

Peter spotted the Pharisee with the golden staff in the crowd. "There he is again. He's probably stirring up more trouble."

"Set Barabbas free! Set Barabbas free!" chanted the crowd.

"Let him go!" Pilate said.

A soldier removed the chains from Barabbas and shoved him down the stairs. Peter watched him disappear into the cheering crowd.

Pilate whispered something to a soldier. The soldier grabbed Jesus and took him down a different set of stairs.

Peter motioned for Mary to follow him as he crept after Jesus. Peter reached the bottom of the stairs and hid behind a thorny bush with pink flowers. Mary and Hank slid in after him.

"*Ouch!*" said Peter. He pulled his sleeve away from the bush and heard a ripping sound. "Those thorns are sharp."

Peter looked through the leaves of the bush and saw soldiers put a purple robe over Jesus' shoulders. A soldier walked their way with his sword drawn.

"Duck!" whispered Peter.

The soldier swung his sword and cut a thorny vine from the bush.

"This should work," said the soldier as he walked away.

Peter saw the soldier wrap the thorny vine into the shape of a crown and shove it on Jesus' head.

Peter squeezed his eyes shut.

"What are they doing?" said Mary.

"Don't look," said Peter.

Peter heard the crack of a whip. Hank whined. Mary hung her head.

The soldiers led Jesus back to Pilate. Peter and

Mary followed at a safe distance as Pilate led Jesus to the top of the stairs. "Behold your King!" shouted Pilate. "What should I do with him?"

"Crucify him! Crucify him!" shouted the crowd.

Pilate motioned to the soldiers. They led Jesus away to the cross.

"Why are they doing this?" said Mary. "He doesn't deserve it."

Peter shook his head. "It looks like Satan's plan is working."

12

IT IS FINISHED

The soldiers led Jesus through the angry mob. Peter and Mary pushed through the crowd after Jesus.

"Crucify him! Crucify him!" the crowd shouted.

Peter saw the soldiers lead Jesus down the road. A huge wooden cross lay in the middle of the street. The soldiers made Jesus pick it up. He carried the cross on his back through the jeering crowd lining the road.

Peter looked down at the ground. It was too hard to watch.

"Look!" said Mary. "There's Sarah."

Ahead, Peter saw Sarah standing next to her parents on the side of the road. Her dad was holding the little, spotted lamb. He motioned to Mary to join Sarah.

Tears rolled down Sarah cheeks. "Why are they doing this to Jesus?" She looked around at the loud, angry crowd. "They wanted him to be king."

Peter heard the crack of a whip. He turned around and saw Jesus stumble and fall under the heavy cross.

A soldier shouted at Jesus to get up, but the weight of the cross was too much.

"Hey, you!" shouted a soldier, pointing at Sarah's dad. "Help him!"

Sarah's dad set the little lamb down and stepped forward.

"No, Simon," said Sarah's mom. "Don't go!"

Sarah's dad looked down at his daughter. A tear fell from his eye. "Jesus helped Sarah. I have to help him."

Sarah's dad walked onto the road. He looked kindly at Jesus and reached out his hand. "Let's go." He grunted as he lifted Jesus and the cross from the dusty road. He looked back at his family. "Wait right here for me."

The cross scraped across the rough road as they dragged it away.

Peter and Mary took turns saying goodbye to Sarah, then hurried out of the city gate after Jesus.

A steep hill made of stones rose up

ahead of Peter. He saw three deep indentions in the side of the hill.

He nudged Mary and pointed. "It looks like a skull."

"Keep moving!" shouted a soldier in the distance.

Peter looked ahead. Sarah's dad and Jesus were struggling to carry the cross up the steep hill. Hank raced ahead while Peter scrabbled up the hill next to Mary.

Jesus and Sarah's dad made it to the top of the hill. They dropped the cross on the hard ground. One of the soldiers nailed a sign to the top of the cross.

"What does it say?" asked Peter.

Mary squinted. "It says, 'Jesus, King of the Jews'."

The soldiers pulled off Jesus' cloak and tossed it on the ground. They laid Jesus on the cross.

Peter saw them take out some spikes and a hammer. He turned away. He didn't want to see Jesus get hurt.

The sound of a hammer rang out across the crowd.

Mary covered her ears and leaned into Peter.

"Woof! Woof!" Hank barked. Peter wrapped his arms around the dog.

The soldiers raised the cross and set it into the ground with a thud.

Peter and Mary watched as two more crosses were raised—one on Jesus' right and one on his left.

Soldiers threw dice on the ground beside Jesus' robe.

"I win!" said one of the soldiers. He picked up the robe.

Mary shook her head and said, "They're acting like this is some kind of game."

Peter looked around at the crowd on the rocky hill. A few people were crying, but most were shouting at Jesus and mocking him. *Why is God letting this happen?* thought Peter.

"Grrrr!" Hank growled at something behind Peter.

Peter turned and saw priests and Pharisees coming up the hill on donkeys. As they rode past, Peter spotted the Pharisee with the golden staff among the men. The Pharisee looked down at Peter. "It looks like my plan is working," he snarled. "Nothing can stop me now!"

"Look at the so-called king!" shouted one of the priests. "He saved others. Why can't he save himself?"

The priests and the Pharisees laughed.

Jesus looked up into the sky. "Father, forgive them. They don't know what they're doing."

One of the men hanging next to Jesus turned

to him. "Aren't you the Christ? Save yourself and save us."

The man on the other cross interrupted him. "We deserve this. He doesn't. Jesus, remember me when you go to your kingdom."

Jesus turned to him. "Today you will be with me in paradise."

Peter heard thunder rumble through the sky. Black clouds rolled in. Darkness covered everything. Peter could barely see ahead of himself.

"What's happening?" Peter whispered to Mary. "It's the middle of the afternoon!"

Jesus cried out, "My God! My God! Why have you abandoned me?"

Peter looked up into the silent sky. *Why wasn't God answering his Son?*

Jesus lowered his head. He looked exhausted and alone.

"How much more can he take?" cried Mary.

Jesus took a rattling breath. "I'm thirsty."

One of the soldiers stuck a sponge on his spear and dipped it in something. He shoved the sponge in Jesus' face.

Jesus raised his head and looked into the dark sky. "Father! Into your hands I give my spirit!"

"Grrrr!" Hank's ears flattened against his head. Peter felt the rocks below his feet rumble. He held onto Mary and looked up at the cross.

Jesus took a deep breath. "It is finished!" He lowered his head. Peter didn't see him breathe again.

13

A Very Sad Day

The rumbling rocks became still. The dark clouds rolled away, and light returned to the hillside. Silence fell on top of the stony hill.

Peter couldn't believe Jesus was dead. He looked at Mary. She was crying. Even Hank whimpered. *Why did God let this happen?* he thought. *Why didn't God send Michael and the angel army to rescue Jesus?*

The soldier who had won Jesus' cloak fell to his knees. He looked up at Jesus' lifeless body as tears filled his eyes. "He truly was the Son of God!"

A man in a fancy robe tapped the soldier on his shoulder. The soldier wiped his eyes and stood up.

"My name is Joseph from Arimathea," said the man in the robe. "Pilate granted me permission to bury Jesus."

Soldiers lowered Jesus' body from the cross and laid him on the ground. A man sprinkled what looked like spices across Jesus' body. Joseph wrapped Jesus in a clean, white cloth. Then two men picked up Jesus and carried him away from the cross.

Peter and Mary plodded slowly after them. They were joined by a group of weeping women.

They came to a small garden beside the hill with a large opening cut into the rocks. It reminded Peter of the place Lazarus had been buried before Jesus raised him from the dead. Peter and Mary waited with the women as Joseph and the other man carried Jesus into the tomb. The men backed out of the tomb and rolled a huge rock over the opening.

The sun began to set. The men and women slowly shuffled out of the garden.

Peter plopped down on the ground. Hank came over and lay beside him.

Mary sat down and rubbed her eyes. "Where do we go now?"

Peter shook his head. "I don't know."

"I guess we'll stay here," said Mary.

Peter lay down and rested his head against the

adventure bag. He stared into the night sky. "The stars don't seem as bright," he said as he drifted off to sleep.

The sun woke Peter early the next morning. His heart sank as he remembered what had happened the day before.

Peter heard his stomach growl. He rummaged through the bag to see if there was any food. He found a couple of apples.

Mary sat up and stretched. "Oh no!"

Peter took a big bite of his apple. "What?"

"We only have two days left to solve the secret of the scroll or we'll be stuck here," said Mary.

"Then we would never see Mom or Dad again," said Peter. He really missed them.

He put the apple down and pulled the scroll out of the bag.

"Let's try to solve it," said Mary.

Peter snapped his fingers. "I've got it," he

said. "Jesus is the Way, the Truth, and the Son of God."

Mary shook her head. "That's too many words."

The scrolls shook. Two words glowed and transformed into the words: AND THE.

"I solved it!" said Peter.

"There's still one more word left," said Mary.

"Well, I almost solved it," said Peter.

Peter and Mary took turns trying to solve the secret all day. Peter guessed words like *Healer* and *King*. Mary guessed words like *Creator* and *Savior*. But none were right.

The sun began to set behind the rocky hill.

"We only have one day left," said Mary.

Peter saw something move out of the corner of his eye. A group of Roman soldiers were marching their way.

Peter shoved the scroll in the bag. "Quick,

hide," he whispered. He pulled Mary behind a flower bush.

"The tomb is right over there," said a voice Peter recognized. He peeked through the flowers and saw the Pharisee with the golden staff walking toward Jesus' tomb.

"Who is it?" said Mary.

"It's Satan," said Peter.

"Make sure the tomb is sealed tight!" said the Pharisee. "We don't want his disciples to steal the body and pretend that he rose from the dead."

One of the soldiers patted the sword hanging by his side. "You can count on me!"

"Your life depends on it," said the Pharisee. "I'll be back to check on the tomb tomorrow."

Peter watched as the priests and Pharisees turned to leave the garden.

"*Grrrr!*" Hank growled.

"*Shhhh,*" said Mary.

The Pharisee with the staff stopped in his tracks. "Go ahead to the Temple without me. I need to check something."

The sound of footsteps grew closer. Peter's heart pounded. Suddenly, something poked him through the bush.

"Come out," snarled the Pharisee. "I know you're there."

Peter crawled out from under the bush. Mary popped out next. Hank snarled at the Pharisee.

The Pharisee smiled. "I'm glad you're here."

"Why?" said Peter.

"So you can see that my plan is working!" He pointed his staff at the tomb. "God's Son is dead!"

The Pharisee slowly walked toward Peter and Mary.

Hank moved in front of them.

"No one can stop me now!" said the Pharisee.

Peter watched an evil grin spread across Satan's face. Peter felt goosebumps on his arms.

"Now I can rule the world!" shouted Satan.

"Don't listen to him," said Mary. "He's a liar."

Peter remembered all the amazing things God had done. He felt his trust in God growing stronger and stronger. "No! Jesus is coming back. He promised to!"

Satan laughed. "He'll never come back! I used my greatest powers—the powers of sin and death!"

Mary shook her head forcefully. "He will come back! And he will defeat you!"

Satan looked around. "I don't see him. I guess that means I win!"

"We believe in Jesus," said Peter. "He will come back to life."

Satan laughed. "I'll see you tomorrow. Maybe Jesus will be alive then." He walked away into the dark night.

14

Endings and Beginnings

The next morning, Peter woke to something poking him in the side. He rubbed his eyes and saw Satan, still wearing his Pharisee disguise, standing above him with his staff. Peter jumped to his feet.

"Good morning!" said Satan.

Now Mary jumped up.

"Grrrr!"

"Good morning to you too," snarled Satan.

"What are you doing here?" said Peter.

"I just wanted to see how Jesus is doing," said Satan.

He walked over to the tomb and greeted the soldiers standing guard. He tapped his staff on the stone in front of the tomb. "Jesus is still dead." Satan raised his arms in victory. "So that means I win! Sin and death win!"

"It's not over yet!" said Peter. "God will win!"

Roar!

The sound came from the tomb. The rocks rumbled and the ground shook.

"What was that?" said Satan.

A ball of light flew through the sky and landed on top of the stone in front of the tomb.

"Michael!" Peter shouted. The angel drew his flaming sword.

The guards backed away from the tomb. Some of the soldiers fainted. The others ran away.

"No!" shouted Satan. "You can't defeat me!" He ran up to the tomb and pushed against the huge rock to hold it in place.

A strong wind blew, and another angel joined Michael. They flew down beside the stone and rolled it away.

Brilliant light blazed from the dark tomb.

Satan fell to the ground and covered his eyes. "No! He's alive!" Satan struggled to his feet. He ran into the garden and disappeared into the shadows.

Jesus walked out of the tomb in a gleaming white robe. Peter heard Mary gasp beside him. He could hardly believe what he was seeing.

Michael and the other angel bowed as Jesus passed them. Jesus walked toward Peter, Mary, and Hank.

As Jesus got closer, Peter could see scars in his hands and feet.

"You're alive!" said Mary.

"I knew you would come back to life!" said Peter. He felt the scroll shake in the adventure bag. He pulled it out.

"Don't open the scroll yet," said Jesus. "I have a few things I want to tell you."

Peter held the scroll by his side and listened.

"Let's take a walk in the garden," said Jesus.

"What about Satan, the Enemy?" said Peter.

"You don't have to worry about him," said Jesus. "I defeated him on the cross."

Peter was confused. "But he thought he defeated you on the cross."

Jesus smiled. "I work in mysterious ways. This was all part of God's plan to rescue his people. I paid the price for sin on the cross and defeated death in the tomb, so you don't have to. Now if anyone believes in me, they can be with me forever."

"You did all of this for us?" said Peter. A tear rolled down his cheek.

Jesus wiped away the tear. "I did it because I love you. Just like I love everyone I created. And I want you to be with me forever."

Jesus looked into Peter's eyes. "Do you believe in me?"

Peter nodded his head. "Yes, I believe."

Jesus smiled and turned to Mary. "Do you believe?"

"Yes, I do," said Mary.

"*Woof! Woof!*" Hank barked and wagged his tail.

"It looks like Hank believes too," said Peter.

Jesus bent over and petted Hank's head. Then Jesus straightened up. "I have a special mission for you. Are you willing to take it?"

Peter and Mary nodded.

"I want you to tell everyone about your adventures and all the amazing things you have seen," said Jesus. "Tell them, so they can believe and be with me forever."

"We will!" said Peter and Mary.

Jesus looked over Peter's shoulder. "More of my friends are coming. It's time for you to solve the secret of the scroll."

"I really miss my parents, but I don't want to leave you," said Mary.

"Don't worry," said Jesus. "I will always be with you."

Peter unrolled the scroll. The last word glowed and transformed into the word: LIFE. Peter read the scroll, "JESUS IS THE WAY, THE TRUTH, AND THE LIFE."

The ground began to shake beneath their feet.

"Wait," said Mary. "Where does the lion's roar come from?"

"It's me," said Jesus. "Remember, I am always with you!"

Everything began to spin around. They landed back in Great-Uncle Solomon's library.

The red wax seal transformed into a gold medallion with a cross inscribed on it. Peter placed it in the adventure bag.

"Let's go tell Great-Uncle Solomon about our adventure!" said Peter.

He raced past Mary out of the library, past the shiny suit of armor, and down the long hallway to the tower. They ran up the spiral stairs and burst into the room. Great-Uncle Solomon looked at both of them and smiled.

They told him about all the amazing things they had seen.

Then Peter noticed the box in the middle of

the table. "Oh yeah. You were going to show us what was in the box."

"You're right," said Great-Uncle Solomon. "I think it might be the last cup Jesus used before his death."

"I can help you know for sure," said Peter.

"You can?" asked Great-Uncle Solomon, "How?"

"I held it," said Peter.

"And dropped it," said Mary.

Great-Uncle Solomon opened the old wooden box and pulled out a dusty clay cup. He gently handed it to Peter.

"Be careful this time," said Mary.

Peter rolled his eyes. "I will." He turned the cup over and brushed away some dust. There was a chip in the bottom of the cup. "It's the one!"

Great-Uncle Solomon clapped his hands. "I knew it!"

"Woof! Woof!"

Hank barked at the tower window. Peter ran over and looked out. "It's Mom and Dad!" he shouted.

Peter bumped into Mary as he raced her down the stairs to the front door. He swung the door open. His parents were standing there with open arms.

His dad beamed. "We're back!"

"We missed you so much!" said his mom.

Peter and Mary ran into their parents' arms for a big, long hug. Hank snuggled in too

Mary wiped a tear from her cheek. "I'm so glad we're finally back together!"

"I hope you didn't get too bored staying with Great-Uncle Solomon," said Dad.

Peter and Mary looked at each other and smiled.

"We have so much to tell you!" said Peter.

Do you want to read more about the events in this story?

The people, places, and events in *The Final Scroll* are drawn from the stories in the Bible. You can read more about them in the following passages in the Bible.

Luke 19:28–40 tells the story of Jesus entering Jerusalem as King.

Matthew 21:12–17 is where you will find Jesus cleansing the Temple.

Mark 14:3–11 tells about Judas's plot to betray Jesus.

Luke 22:7–53 tells the story of the Last Supper and Jesus being arrested.

Matthew 26:57–75 describes Jesus' trial before the High Priest and Simon Peter's denial of Jesus.

John 18:28–19:16 tells about Jesus' trial before Pilate.

Luke 23:26–49 tells the story of Jesus being crucified.

Matthew 27:62–28:20 is where you will find the exciting story of Jesus' resurrection!

Special Note:
Sarah is a fictional character representing children in Jerusalem during the life of Jesus.

CATCH ALL
PETER AND MARY'S ADVENTURES!

In **The Beginning**, Peter, Mary, and Hank witness the Creation of the earth while battling a sneaky snake.

In **Race to the Ark**, the trio must rush to help Noah finish the ark before the coming flood.

In **The Great Escape**, Peter, Mary, and Hank journey to Egypt and see the devastation of the plagues.

In **Journey to Jericho**, the trio lands in Jericho as the Israelites prepare to enter the Promised Land.

In ***The Shepherd's Stone***, Peter, Mary, and Hank accompany David as he prepares to fight Goliath.

In ***The Lion's Roar***, the trio arrive in Babylon and uncover a secret plot to get Daniel thrown in the lions' den.

In ***The King Is Born***, Peter, Mary, and Hank visit Bethlehem at the time of Jesus' birth.

In ***Miracles by the Sea***, the trio meets Jesus and the disciples and witnesses amazing miracles.

In ***The Final Scroll***, Peter, Mary, and Hank travel back to Jerusalem and witness Jesus' crucifixion and resurrection.

ABOUT THE AUTHOR

 Mike Thomas grew up in Florida playing sports and riding his bike to the library and the arcade. He graduated from Liberty University, where he earned a bachelor's degree in Bible Studies.

When his son Peter was nine years old, Mike went searching for books that would teach Peter about the Bible in a fun and imaginative way. Finding none, he decided to write his own series. In The Secret of the Hidden Scrolls, Mike combines biblical accuracy with adventure, imagination, and characters who are dear to his heart. The main characters are named after Mike's son Peter, his niece Mary, and his dog, Hank.

Mike lives in Tennessee with his wife, Lori; two sons, Payton and Peter; and Hank.

For more information about the author and the series, visit www.secretofthehiddenscrolls.com.